For Hairy Toes,
Furry Paws
and Arthur

This book belongs to:

Sneaky Weasel ☙ ESQ

and

KEEP OFF!

THIS IS A BORZOI BOOK PUBLISHED BY ALFRED A. KNOPF

Copyright © 2008 by Hannah Shaw

All rights reserved. Published in the United States by Alfred A. Knopf,
an imprint of Random House Children's Books,
a division of Random House, Inc., New York.

Originally published in Great Britain in 2008 by Jonathan Cape, an imprint of Random House Children's Books.

Knopf, Borzoi Books, and the colophon are registered trademarks of Random House, Inc.

Visit us on the Web! www.randomhouse.com/kids

Educators and librarians, for a variety of teaching tools,
visit us at www.randomhouse.com/teachers

Library of Congress Cataloging-in-Publication Data is available on request.

ISBN 978-0-375-85625-9 (trade) ISBN 978-0-375-95625-6 (lib. bdg.)

The illustrations in this book were created using a combination of pen and ink, printmaking techniques, and Photoshop.

MANUFACTURED IN MALAYSIA

February 2009

10 9 8 7 6 5 4 3 2 1

First American Edition

Sneaky Weasel

REAL
LIFE
STORY

THIS
WEEK:

"HOW I
OVERCAME
MY FEAR OF
PENCILS"
- RABBIT

ROGUE
MAGAZINE

MR SNEAKY WEASEL

It's the
Weasel who
thinks he
has everything!

THE
BAD
CATS
GUIDE

Hannah Shaw

ALFRED A. KNOPF — NEW YORK

Weasel was sneaky.

He was a bully and a cheat
– a nasty, measly Weasel.

His *mean* schemes and *cunning* tricks
had made him *richer* than
you can possibly imagine.

One day Weasel decided to throw a party to boast about his incredible castle, fast car and **huge** swimming pool.

He sent off invitations to everyone he could think of.

invitation

S✦W

Dear friends,

I, Sneaky Weasel, invite you — yes, *you* — to a party.

I am very rich and important, so don't be late.

Signed,

S. Weasel **ESQ**

S. Weasel ESQ. at Weasel Towers

P.S. Watch out, the crocodiles in the moat might be hungry!

Rat

On *the day* of the party
Weasel dressed in his finest clothes
and admired himself in the mirror.

"Don't I look *handsome*?"
he asked his reflection.

Then Weasel waited expectantly for his guests to arrive.

He waited…

and Waited…

But no one came.

Being rich and powerful isn't much fun when there's no one to impress.

"Why would anyone NOT want to come to my party?" sulked Weasel.

"I will visit them all and demand an explanation."

First, Weasel went to see Rabbit. He banged on the door.
When Rabbit saw Weasel, he started *shaking*.
"What's the matter with *you*?" Said Weasel crossly.
"And *why* didn't you come to *my* party?"

Next, Weasel went to see Rat in his *laboratory*.
"Why didn't *you* come to my party?"
he snapped.

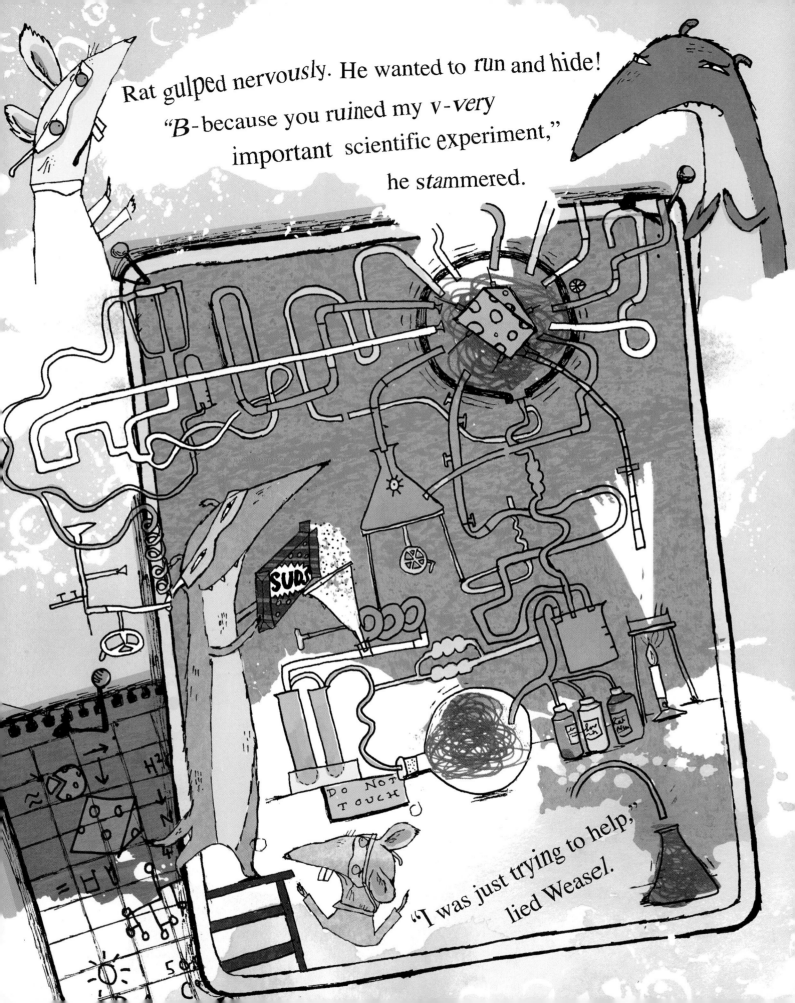

Off Weasel went to visit Hedgehog,
but on the way he met Hedgehog's mum.
"Hedgehog isn't *very* well," she said.

"He's been scratching for days and days and he just can't stop."

"Ah," said Weasel, feeling a bit itchy himself.

Weasel was starting to feel quite *guilty*,
so he *crept* past Shrew's house.

"Not so *fast*," said a little voice.

"It was a joke," protested Weasel. "My cat only likes caviar, he wouldn't eat you."

"Well it wasn't funny," squeaked Shrew.

"Nobody came to your party because you're mean and nasty and a bad friend. And you never ever say sorry!"

Weasel went *home* feeling m*ea*sly.
He had been a *horrible* bully.

"I *must* f*in*d a way to be a *good* friend,"
he thought desperately,

"but h*ow*?"

Weasel paced **round** and **round** all night,
trying to think of good ideas.
This wasn't *easy* because
most of *his* thoughts were *wickedly* sneaky,
but by morning he had a pla*n* . . .

weasels
BEING GOOD PLAN

Weasel cookies

"What I need to do," said Weasel,
"is put right everything I've done wrong."

So that is exactly what he did.

Everyone was pleased that Weasel was making *such* an effort.

"But there is still one thing we *haven't* heard you say," said Shrew.

Weasel thought long and hard. After a while, he began to mumble,

"I'm *so . . . so* important! No . . . I'm *su . . .* super sneaky?"

The other animals began to laugh.

"I've got *it!*" cried Weasel.

"I'm Sorry!"

"Hurray!" they all cheered.

Weasel decided to throw a party to celebrate being good at being good.

This time, everyone came.

"Yippee!" cried Weasel.

"Let's party!"

And *I*'d like to say that Weasel *finally* learned
the error of his ways and stopped being sneaky altogether.

But *sometimes* he just couldn't help himself . . .